KING KONG

Adapted by
Judith Conaway

**Conceived by Edgar Wallace
and Merian C. Cooper**

Novelization by Delos W. Lovelace

Text illustrations by Paul Van Munching

Cover illustration by Glenn Dean

STEP-UP CLASSIC CHILLERS™

RANDOM HOUSE 🏠 NEW YORK

Library of Congress Cataloging-in-Publication Data:
Conaway, Judith. 1948— .
   King Kong / adapted by Judith Conaway : conceived by Edgar Wallace and Merian C. Cooper : novelization by Delos W. Lovelace : text illustrations by Paul Van Munching.
       p. cm.—(Step-up classic chillers)
   SUMMARY: A young film actress on location on a remote jungle island is chosen by the natives to be the bride of their giant gorilla god Kong.
   [1. Gorillas—Fiction. 2. Monsters—Fiction. 3. Motion pictures—Fiction.] I. Van Munching, Paul, ill. II. Lovelace, Delos Wheeler, 1894–1967. King Kong. III. Title. IV. Series. PZ7.C7575Ki 1988
[Fic]—dc19 87-28354   ISBN: 0-394-89789-7 (pbk.)

Manufactured in the United States of America   4 5 6 7 8 9 0

Chapter 1

The sky was growing dark. A thin veil of snow was falling on New York City. The streets were crowded with people. Old ladies with shopping bags. Young couples out on dates. People leaving work. The city was a never-ending tide of human beings.

One person seemed to be swimming against the tide. He was dressed like a banker. But you could tell that he had not spent his life behind a desk. He looked healthy and strong.

The man's name was Carl Denham. He was a movie director. The craziest movie man in Hollywood, people said. Denham went to distant places where there was great danger. Places like Africa and New Guinea. Now people were whispering about Denham's next picture. It was going to be his most dangerous yet, they said.

The truth was even wilder than people thought. Denham was ready to leave for his next location. He had a ship waiting at the New Jersey docks. It was due to sail at six the next morning. In fact, if the ship *didn't* sail, there would be trouble. The insurance people wanted to talk to Denham. They had heard there were guns and gas bombs on board.

But Denham still did not have a young woman to act in his picture. It was going to be the best movie he

ever made. But it needed a young woman.

Denham had tried every acting agency in New York. They had all turned him down.

"You take too many chances," people had said. "And you won't even tell us where you're going. No actress will take the job."

That was why Denham was walking the streets of New York. He was looking for the right face for his picture. He looked into thousands of faces. Faces on park benches. Faces in bread lines. Sad faces, happy faces. But not one was *the* face for his greatest movie ever.

Denham sighed. He was getting tired. He turned to walk down Broadway. The afternoon shows would be getting out. There would be thousands of new faces. But first, thought Denham, he would have a cup of coffee.

There was a tiny food counter at the next corner. Denham squeezed himself in. He stood between a pile of apples and a stack of cups. "Coffee, black. To go," he said. He looked down at the apples.

That was when he saw the hand. It was a very pretty hand. And it was about to snatch one of the apples.

Another hand clamped down on the first. "Aha!" yelled the shop-keeper. "I caught you, you thief! I'll call the cops."

"No!" cried the young woman. "Please let me go. I didn't take anything!"

"It's true," Denham said. "She didn't touch those apples." He gave the shopkeeper a dollar. "Here, take this. That should take care of it."

The young woman looked up at Denham. "Thank you, sir," she said. It was then that Denham first saw her face. It was the face he was looking for!

Half an hour later Denham and the young woman were sitting in a restaurant. The woman had a pile of empty plates in front of her. She had just finished her first good meal in weeks.

She put down her coffee cup. "I'm a different Ann Darrow now," she said. "Thank you, sir."

"How did you get into such a fix?" asked Denham.

"Bad luck, that's all." Ann smiled sadly. "The old story. No money, couldn't find a job. It happens to

10

hundreds of people. There's a depression going on, you know."

Denham could not stop looking at her. She was more than beautiful. Her face had all the best angles for the camera. And those clear blue eyes! That glowing skin! That long golden hair! She was a movie director's dream come true.

"Ever do any acting?" Denham asked.

"I've been an extra a few times," she answered. "Once I even had a real part."

"And are you the sort of girl who is afraid of mice and snakes?"

Ann looked at him, puzzled.

"I'm Carl Denham," he explained. "Ever heard of me?"

"Y-yes," Ann replied. "You make moving pictures. In jungles and places."

"That's me. And I've picked you to star in my next picture. We sail at six."

Ann gaped at him.

"Don't just sit there, Ann," Denham said. "Come on. We've got only a few hours to get you some new clothes."

Chapter 2

Ann Darrow opened her eyes. What was different? She was not feeling hungry. It was the first morning in a long time that her stomach was not empty.

She saw a bowl of apples next to her bed. Then she remembered. She sat up, looked around, and laughed out loud. She had not been dreaming after all!

She was in a cabin, on a ship called the *Wanderer*. Her room was rocking up and down. And the engines hummed under her feet. They had already left land far behind them!

Then Ann saw the boxes. She laughed again. There were dress boxes and hat boxes and shoe boxes. There were enough jars and bottles to fill a beauty shop. To someone as poor as Ann those boxes were the most beautiful sight in the world.

Ann spent more than an hour getting dressed. She could not believe her luck. Yesterday she had been dressed in rags. She had been so hungry that she had been ready to steal. Today she was well-dressed and well-fed. And she had a job!

True, Denham had not told her where they were going. But Ann felt sure that she could trust him. And hadn't she always dreamed of adventure?

Smiling to herself, Ann left her

cabin and set out to explore the ship.

The deck was almost empty. The only person in sight was an old sailor. He was sunning himself and playing with a monkey. The old sailor gave Ann a friendly smile.

"Mornin'," he said. "Me, I'm Lumpy. This here's Ignatz."

"Ann Darrow," said Ann. She shook hands with both of them. Then she sat down and stretched in the warm sun.

A sharp whistle blew. Lumpy jumped to his feet. The monkey hopped into Ann's lap. She smiled at her new little friend.

Suddenly the deck was full of sailors. One young man seemed to be their leader. He was the one who had blown the whistle. The young man did not notice Ann.

But Ann certainly noticed him. She thought he was the best-looking man she had ever seen. She liked his strong, dark face. She liked the muscles that rippled across his shoulders.

Ann remembered what Denham had told her about the people on board. This must be Jack Driscoll, the first mate.

Driscoll still had not seen Ann. He stood with his back to her. As he shouted orders he stepped back. Soon he was quite close to Ann.

A sailor dropped a rope. "Don't put it there," called Driscoll. "It goes back *here*." He swung back his arm. His hand hit Ann in the face!

"What . . . ?" Driscoll wheeled around. His eyes started when he saw Ann. "Oh! I'm so sorry! I hope I didn't hurt you."

"Oh, not at all," said Ann politely. They both laughed.

"You're sure it doesn't hurt?"

"I can stand it," Ann replied. Then in a sad voice she added, "Life's been mostly socks in the jaw for me."

Jack looked at her quickly. "We'll have to do something about that," he said. Their eyes met. It was a long time before either one of them looked away.

Chapter 3

The days glided by. Ann loved life aboard the *Wanderer*. The rest, fresh air, and good food made her feel like a new person. Her sad days of being poor seemed far behind.

Work on the movie was going well. Ann spent hours each day in front of Denham's camera. The director tested her face from every angle. He was delighted. This would be his greatest picture yet. Ann was perfect!

The sailors thought Ann was perfect too. She had won the heart of every man on board. She was a real lady, they said. Always had a kind word for everyone.

Even Captain Englehorn had fallen for her. He was a tough old sailor. But in front of Ann he became a different person.

"Isn't the captain a sweet old lamb?" Ann said to Jack Driscoll one day.

"A *what*?" Driscoll laughed. "Don't ever let anyone else hear you call him that, Ann. Englehorn would never live it down."

Ann and Jack were now close friends. Jack was not used to women. But he found Ann easy to talk to. He told her all about his life. How he had run away from college to go to sea. How his mother had finally forgiven him. How he had met Denham.

Ann told her story too. Her mother

and father had been killed in a car accident. They had left her a rich young woman. But an uncle had cheated her out of her money. She had gone to New York to look for work.

"I was down to my last penny when I met Denham," Ann said. "That was my lucky day."

Jack Driscoll was not so sure. He was worried. He knew how wild his boss's ideas could be. And Denham still had not told them where they were going.

They had sailed through the Panama Canal. Hawaii was behind them. So was Japan. So were the Philippines and Ceylon. Still no word from Denham. Jack decided it was time to have a talk.

He went right over to Denham.

"Look here," Jack said. "You've got to let me know what we're in for. Where are we heading? What crazy plans do you have this time?"

Denham raised an eyebrow. "What's this, Jack? You going soft on me?"

"You know I'm not," Driscoll said. "It's Ann. . . ."

"Oh!" said Denham. "So you've gone soft on *her*." He frowned. "As if I haven't got enough problems without you falling in love."

"Who said anything about love?" cried Jack. His face was red.

"I always thought you were a real tough guy, Jack," Denham went on. "But if Beauty gets you. . . ." He laughed. "It's just like my movie. The Beast is a tough guy. Tougher than anyone. He can lick the world. But when Beauty comes along, she gets him."

"What are you talking about?" asked Driscoll.

The director laughed again. "Come on, Jack. Let's go see Englehorn. It's time I gave you both some answers."

They found Captain Englehorn in the chart room. He was looking at a big map. "Here we are, Denham," he said, pointing. "You promised me some facts when we got to this point. So tell me where we go from here."

"Southwest," snapped Denham.

"Southwest?" said Englehorn. "But—there's nothing there!"

"Nothing but *this*!" cried Denham. He took a piece of paper out of his pocket. "I got this map from an old sea captain. A man I trust. He's not the sort to spin tales. So I know this place is real."

Denham spread the paper in front of them. They gasped in astonishment.

The map showed an island. At one end was a strip of sand in the shape of a finger. It was about a mile long.

In the center of the island was a huge mountain. It was shaped like a skull. All around the skull were steep cliffs. The cliffs were covered with thick jungle.

The most amazing detail on the map was a wall. It rose between the sand "finger" and the jungle-covered cliffs.

"And what a wall!" said Denham. "It is higher than twenty tall men. And it's hundreds of years old. The natives of the island are savages.

They don't know when the wall was built. Or by whom. But they keep the wall strong, just the same."

"Why?" Jack wanted to know.

"Because there's something on the other side," answered Denham. "Something they fear." He lowered his voice. "Have either of you ever heard of . . . Kong?"

Driscoll shook his head. But Captain Englehorn nodded slowly. "Kong? Why, yes. The Malay people talk about him. Some kind of god or devil, isn't he?"

"He's something, all right," said Denham. "Something huge. And powerful. He holds that island in a grip of fear. And I am going to find the beast and take his picture."

Jack Driscoll gulped. The Beast! Denham's movie was about Beauty and the Beast. Ann Darrow's lovely face appeared before him.

Suddenly, for the first time in his life, Jack Driscoll was afraid.

Chapter 4

Jack pushed up the floor plate of the crow's-nest. He climbed up. Then he reached down to Ann. He helped her climb up too. The trap door dropped shut. They were in a little world of their own, high above the water.

Ann looked out over the blue ocean. The sun sparkled on the waves. "How wonderful!" Ann cried. "Why didn't you bring me up here sooner? Why, from up here I might even see Denham's island."

She looked at Driscoll. "Do you think we'll find the place?"

"I hope not," Jack said.

"Why, shame on you!" Ann teased. "To think you ran away from home for a life of adventure."

Driscoll looked into her eyes. "You know why I'm worried, Ann."

Ann pretended not to hear him. "Look, Jack!" she said. "Here's Ignatz, coming up to join us." The monkey scampered up the ropes. Soon it was sitting on Ann's shoulder.

"Ann, look at me!" begged Jack. But she was busy playing with the monkey.

"Please, Ann! We have so little time. You know I'm scared for you. You know—I love you!"

Ann looked at him. She could pretend no longer. She moved into Jack's arms.

Ignatz screeched. The lovers did

not hear. They did not see the red and orange sunset either. Or the fog that was creeping toward the ship.

All through the night the fog grew thicker. By morning the ship was wrapped in a yellow blanket. They had slowed down to a crawl.

Denham, Driscoll, and Ann were standing with the captain. They could hardly keep still. They were getting near the island at last!

From down below came the voice of a sailor. He was measuring the depth of the water.

"Thirty fathoms!" he called. "Twenty-five fathoms! Twenty fathoms! Ten!"

"We're closing in fast," said the captain. "Better tell them to drop anchor, Jack."

Driscoll gave the order. They heard the anchor splash into the water. At the same moment they heard another sound too.

"Drums!" Englehorn said.

As they listened a wind came up. The fog parted like a curtain. And

there was the island. It was less than a quarter of a mile away.

"Skull Mountain!" shouted Denham. "Do you see it? And the wall! The wall!" He was jumping for joy. "Get out the boats!" he cried. "Everybody to shore!"

Chapter 5

They were on the beach in less than an hour. Denham brought his camera along. Ann came too. She was already in costume for the movie. Denham did not want to miss any chance for a single shot.

Jack thought Ann ought to stay behind. "Let's go first, just to make sure it's safe," he said.

"Don't worry, Jack," said Denham. "We've got enough guns and gas bombs for an army."

They did look a bit like an army as they landed on the island. They had two boats. Each one carried twenty men. Each man carried a rifle. Some men also carried the bombs. Others had movie equipment.

There was not a soul in sight. The drums grew louder and louder.

"They must be having some sort of ceremony," Denham said.

Suddenly loud voices rose above the drums, repeating the word "Kong."

"Listen!" said Ann. "They're calling for Kong."

"Stay here," said Denham. "I'll move up ahead and see what's going on."

He was back in a flash. "Everybody keep quiet!" he hissed. "Get the cameras rolling! And follow me!"

They crept ahead.

In front of them lay a great square.

The square was packed with people. Their bodies were painted in bright colors. They were all dancing and chanting "Kong."

At the far end of the square was the wall. In the wall was a huge gate. Heavy stone steps led up to the gate. A beautiful young girl was kneeling on the top step. She was wearing a necklace of flowers.

Drummers stood in a row on both sides of the kneeling girl. Over to the left a witch doctor danced. Over to the right was a big man sitting on a throne. He wore bright feathers. He was clearly the chief.

By this time Denham had his cameras going. This was better than he could ever have hoped for. What a movie this would be!

Suddenly the drumbeats changed. Six big men leaped up onto the steps. They were all dressed like gorillas. The people chanted louder than ever.

"Kong! Kong! Kong!"

Now it was the chief's turn to enter the dance. He stood up. But he never began his part. For at that moment he saw the strangers.

"Bado!" he shouted. *"Bado! Dama pati vego!"*

The drums stopped. The chanting stopped. The people stood still. There was dead silence.

"Easy, boys," said Denham. "Remember, we're the ones with the guns. Don't make any sudden moves."

The chief waved his hand. The women and children left the square. Only the kneeling girl stayed. The men raised their spears.

"Watu!" shouted the chief. *"Tama di? Tama di?"*

"We're in luck," said Captain Englehorn. "I can talk their lingo." He stepped forward.

"Greetings!" he called. "We are your friends! *Bala! Bala!* Friends!"

The chief did not seem to need more friends. *"Tasko! Tasko!"* he yelled.

"That means beat it," said Englehorn.

"Talk him out of it," Denham ordered. "Ask him what this dance is all about."

Englehorn spoke to the chief and pointed to the kneeling girl. The chief's answer did not make Englehorn happy.

"The chief says she is the bride of Kong," he said.

The sailors all had the same thought. They moved into a group around Ann Darrow. But it was too late. The witch doctor had already seen her.

"Malem!" he screamed. *"Malem me pakeno! Kow bisa para Kong!"*

"The woman of gold!" Englehorn said. "That witch doctor wants Ann. I'll bet he's never seen anyone with blond hair before. He says that he will trade six women for her."

"Tell him it's no deal," said Denham. "But try and be nice about it."

The captain and the chief spoke a few more words.

"I told him we would talk more tomorrow," said Captain Englehorn.

"Then let's get back to the ship now," Denham ordered. "We'll go slowly. With big smiles on our faces. You men there. You go first. Keep Ann in the middle. And keep your guns ready."

They did as Denham told them. Soon they were back in the boats. They headed quickly for the ship.

Ann was the first to get her voice back. "Wow!" she said. "I don't know about the rest of you. But I wouldn't have missed that for anything!"

Chapter 6

The sky grew pink and then red. The sun went down. Night blackened the sky. But still the drums kept beating.

It was not a pleasant sound to the people out on the *Wanderer*. They were all a little afraid. What dangers would tomorrow bring?

Ann was sitting up on the deck with old Lumpy. As usual, the monkey, Ignatz, was running about.

"I hear you had quite a time of it ashore, Miss Ann," said Lumpy. "You broke up a wedding party, they say."

"Oh, Lumpy!" said Ann. "It was *so*

exciting! The bride of Kong! Who *is* Kong, do you suppose?"

"Aw, just an old log or a mud statue," answered Lumpy. "Some nonsense. All these tribes believe in witches and ghosts. Not a word of truth in any of it, if you ask me."

"Maybe you're right," Ann replied. She moved her foot. Without meaning to, she stepped on Ignatz's tail. The monkey squealed and ran away.

"That varmint!" cried Lumpy. "I'll catch him!" He ran after his pet.

Ann stood up and stretched. The night air was making her feel sleepy. She yawned, looking around the deck. No one else was about.

Suddenly a hand clamped over Ann's open mouth! Someone grabbed her from behind! Ann twisted and struggled. But it was no use.

She was a prisoner of the savages of Skull Mountain Island!

Ann felt herself being lifted over the ship's rail. More hands grabbed her and pulled her down into the bottom of a canoe. All this time the hand was still pressed over her mouth. Ann could not make a sound.

The canoe reached the shore. Ann was so afraid that she could not move her legs. Two of the savages picked her up and carried her.

Soon they were back in the great square. Again the square was packed with people. They chanted and danced in the torchlight. The drums beat.

Ann looked out over the many faces. One face stood out from the others. It was the girl who had been kneeling on the steps that afternoon.

But now she was dressed like all the other women.

Ann felt herself being carried up steps. A necklace of flowers was placed over her head. Six men dressed like gorillas began to dance around her.

Only then did the truth hit her. She, Ann Darrow, had taken the girl's place. *She* was the new bride of Kong!

Ann screamed. Then her fear overcame her, and everything went black.

Chapter 7

Old Lumpy sounded the alarm. It had taken him ten minutes to catch Ignatz. Then he took the monkey back to Ann. But Ann wasn't there.

The old man was puzzled. He walked back along the deck. His foot hit something. It was a bracelet of feathers!

"On deck!" Lumpy shouted. "All hands on deck!"

The men hurried up from below. Denham and Driscoll came running.

"Look!" Lumpy shouted, holding the bracelet. "Them savages have been here. And I don't see Miss Ann!"

A quick search told them the worst. Ann was gone!

"To the boats!" yelled Denham. "I want a rifle for every man! And don't forget the gas bombs!"

The sailors raced for the shore. As they landed, Ann's scream cut the air. They ran toward the sound.

They got to the square. There was Ann at the far end. Not a moment to lose! The big gate was opening! The gorilla men were picking Ann up! They were carrying her through the gate! The sailors charged through the rows of drummers and dancers.

But they didn't make it. The gorilla men came dancing back in. Ann was not with them. The great gate swung shut.

Clang!

A metal gong sounded. The drums and chants stopped. The natives ran for the wall. They used ropes to pull themselves up. Soon the whole tribe was standing along the top. Once again they began to chant.

"Kong! Kong! Kong! Kong!"

Ann was dreaming that she stood on a high, windy place. Her hands were tied. Around her were flames.

She opened her eyes. The memories came back. It wasn't a dream!

She was tied to a high stone altar. The altar was lit by four torches.

A shadow fell over her. A blood-curdling roar filled the night air. The most horrifying beast she had ever seen came crashing out of the jungle.

It was Kong!

Kong was a gigantic gorilla. He was as tall as twenty men. And as wide. The great beast stood up on his toes. He pounded his chest and roared again. He screamed at the people on the wall.

Then Kong saw Ann and his roar stopped.

Why, what was this? Something golden. Something he had never seen before. His huge furry hand touched Ann's hair.

The natives waited, hoping. Would Kong accept the woman of gold? Yes! He was tearing the ropes that held her! Kong was picking her up! Once more they took up their chant.

Instead of harming Ann, Kong handled her very gently. He patted her hair again. His face was full of wonder. He carefully placed Ann into the crook of his arm.

A gunshot whistled past Kong's ear. The gorilla didn't notice. Kong's only thought was of his new treasure. So he did not notice the gate opening either. He did not see the men who slipped through.

Kong gave another roar. He turned. Then he crashed back into the jungle.

Chapter 8

Jack Driscoll was the one who had fired the gun. He was the leader now.

"I'm going in to get Ann back!" cried Jack. "I'll need a dozen men. Who's coming with me?"

"I'll go!" cried one of the men. The others called out the same.

Driscoll chose the ten best men. He and Denham made twelve. The men armed themselves with guns and gas bombs.

"We'll leave you in charge here, Englehorn," said Denham. The captain nodded. He handed out guns to the men who were staying behind.

By this time the natives had disappeared. They were hiding in their houses. They were afraid. What kind of devils were these men who had come to their island? What men would dare to hunt the great Kong?

The search party set out. At first it was easy going. Their flashlights followed the path. They passed the great altar. Then the trail stopped. They were up against a high cliff.

"I hear a waterfall," said Denham. "Let's find it. Maybe we can follow the water and find a way up this cliff." They made their way toward the sound.

They found the stream. The water shot down the cliff in a long slide. Sure enough, there was a narrow path next to the water.

"Here's a track!" called one of the men. They shone their flashlights. It was a gigantic footprint. In fact, four men could lie down in it.

The men found more tracks and followed them up the path. It was a rough climb. But at last they pulled themselves up to the top of the cliff.

Now their real troubles began. They were in a thick, dark jungle. Huge trees arched over their heads. Their flashlights were useless little stabs into the darkness.

There was no trail, so they followed the stream. They began to climb again. Soon they found more giant footprints.

Up and up they climbed. At last they heard a welcome sound. Birds called to each other. Daylight was coming!

"We'll really pick up speed now," said Denham.

The sun rose. The men found themselves in a big open meadow. Ahead of them something moved. One of the men gave a cry of fear.

An enormous animal came crashing out of the jungle. It had thick, scaly skin and a long, spiked tail.

"Quick!" shouted Jack. "The gas bombs! And when I throw, everybody hit the dirt!"

He threw a bomb at the monster. Clouds of gas covered the beast. The men dived for cover.

They heard the giant footsteps coming closer. Closer. Then the footsteps stopped. The ground shook as the monster fell dead.

The men crowded around for a close look. They could not believe

what they saw. "It's a prehistoric beast!" said Denham. "A dinosaur! These animals have been extinct for millions of years."

"Not on Skull Mountain Island," Driscoll replied. "Here the past is still alive. Why, Kong must be a prehistoric animal too. This island could be swarming with monsters."

The men looked at one another. They shivered. But Ann was still Kong's prisoner. So there was nothing they could do but go on.

Chapter 9

Soon the men picked up Kong's tracks again. The big gorilla was still following the stream. After a while the trail began to slope down. They walked into a small valley. A cloud of fog rose to meet them.

The stream got wider. It turned into a small lake. The men stopped at the water's edge. They could hear Kong splashing up ahead.

"Kong's swimming across," said Driscoll. "But we can't swim it. Not with these bombs and guns. We'll have to build a raft."

The sailors worked quickly. They cut down trees. They tied them together with vines. In no time they had the guns and bombs on board. There was barely enough room for the men to squeeze on.

They had a terrible time. The raft leaned first to one side and then to the other. Even so, they rowed almost the whole way across.

But then they hit something. And the thing moved!

"A dinosaur!" cried Denham. "Look! Another dinosaur!"

A huge, scaly body with a snakelike head and neck rose out of the water beneath the raft. The raft was tossed into the air. The men were thrown into the water with the guns and bombs. The men swam hard for the shore.

Jack Driscoll got there first. He pulled himself up onto the bank. He looked over his shoulder. The dinosaur was coming after them! Driscoll got to his feet and started running.

Now the trail led up a hill. Driscoll charged. He ran until he reached the top. Denham was right behind him. The other men caught up with them, one by one.

But the last man did not make it. The dinosaur caught him. The poor man died in the dinosaur's jaws.

The others huddled together for comfort. They looked at the trail ahead.

In front of them lay a wide, flat plain. The whole plain was black. Some parts of it were an inky ooze. Other parts were hard, black rock.

"It's asphalt," said Driscoll. "As

thick as mud. We'll never get across."

Suddenly there was Kong! He appeared at the other side of the black plain. He began to walk toward the men. Kong was still carrying Ann gently in the crook of his arm. Her bright golden hair tumbled down over his dark fur.

"Look!" one of the men whispered. "Look at what's following Kong!"

Three horrible beasts were right behind the great gorilla! They were short, ugly monsters with thick necks and heads. Each head had three sharp horns.

"Triceratopses!" whispered Denham. "More prehistoric beasts!"

Suddenly Kong took Ann out of his arm. He placed her gently up in a tall tree. Then, without warning, he turned.

Kong attacked first. The triceratopses did not have a chance. Kong picked up huge chunks of asphalt. With enormous power he hurled them down on the horrible horns.

One of the monsters fell. Then another. Kong roared in triumph. He beat his chest with his giant fists.

The last triceratops gave up. Slowly it backed away from Kong.

"It's coming our way!" Driscoll said. "Move! Over there, to the right!"

They moved quickly. But once again the last man did not make it. He stumbled and fell. The triceratops caught him. Its horn went right through his chest.

Now the rest of the men were standing at the edge of a ravine—a deep hole in the earth. They could see dark shapes crawling around in the blackness far below.

A log lay across the ravine. It was the only way to get to the other side. And they had to cross. The triceratops was behind them.

Jack Driscoll jumped onto the log. The others followed. This time Denham was the last man.

Driscoll made it across. The others got to the middle of the log. Then they froze. Kong!

The gorilla's roar split the air. Kong had leaped across the ravine! Now he stood behind Jack! The men were trapped! They screamed in fear.

Kong stomped to the edge of the ravine. Jack grabbed a vine and began to climb down the ravine. He found a hole in the side and hid. Denham ran back to the other side and hid too—just in time. Kong picked up the log and began to swing it back and forth.

The men hung on as long as they could. But one by one they fell screaming to their deaths.

Now there were only two of them. Denham stood on one side of the ravine. Jack Driscoll peered out from the hole on the other side. Denham was safe for now. The triceratops had run away at Kong's roar. But Jack was in trouble. Kong had seen him!

Kong's great hairy hands reached into the hole where Jack was hiding. Jack stabbed Kong's fingers with his knife. Kong howled in pain and anger.

There was an answering scream. "Help! He-e-e-e-lp!" It was Ann!

Kong wheeled around. He leaped across the ravine again. He crashed back to the tree where he had left Ann. A huge dinosaur was coming toward her. Ann screamed again.

Kong forgot all about Jack Driscoll. Here was someone trying to steal his prize! Kong went for the monster's throat.

It was a terrible, bloody fight. Both

monsters were about the same size. The dinosaur had long, sharp teeth and powerful hind legs.

But Kong was the smarter fighter. Again and again he tricked the other beast into moving. Then Kong charged. On his last charge, Kong tore apart the dinosaur's jaws.

Then Kong sat down next to the body. He made happy little sounds. He looked up at Ann. He seemed to want her to praise him for protecting her. But Ann lay still. Once again she had passed out from fear.

Kong picked her up carefully. He laid her head gently upon his great shoulder. Then he set off again through the jungle.

Chapter 10

Driscoll and Denham faced each other across the ravine.

"You go back!" shouted Jack. "Get more men! Get more bombs! I'll stay on Kong's trail. I'll mark the path for you and the others."

Denham nodded. Jack was right. The two of them did not stand a chance against Kong. And someone had to keep Ann in sight.

"Good luck, Jack!" Denham called. He waved. Then Denham turned and ran as he had never run before.

As he ran he thought of the men

that he had lost. Tears came to his eyes. He ran harder. He hardly noticed the vines that scratched his face. He hardly noticed the sharp rocks cutting his feet.

Denham got back to the village that night. By this time he was bone tired. He could hardly drag himself along.

Two sailors stood guard at the gate. They saw Denham coming. They ran out to help him.

"What happened, Chief? Where are the rest of them?"

Their faces grew sad as Denham told his story.

"I'm going right back in there!" Denham cried. "Who will come with me? I can't promise anything but danger. Maybe even death."

"I'll go!" cried Lumpy.

"I'll go too," said Captain Englehorn. "There's not a man here who wouldn't. But nobody's going anywhere until morning. We won't get anywhere if we try again tonight. We'll make up the lost time by daylight."

Denham had to agree. The plan made sense. He sat down to eat and rest. But he could not sleep.

Meanwhile, Jack Driscoll was following Kong.

The gorilla seemed to have forgotten all about the men. He charged on. Kong seemed to be following no trail. Instead he zigzagged back and forth. The trail grew even steeper.

It was a hard climb for Jack. He was hungry and tired. But Kong seemed to go faster with every step. Jack saw that they were now climbing up the back of Skull Mountain.

"Kong is heading for home," thought Jack. It made sense. Kong was the only monster on the island who could climb. Up here he was safe from the dinosaurs and water beasts. From up here he could rule his island-kingdom.

Now and then Jack could hear the sound of running water. Suddenly he came upon an amazing sight. A jet of water shot right out of the side of Skull Mountain. Jack looked back down. It was the same stream that they had been following all along!

Jack climbed on. He could hardly pull himself up now. He gave one last push. Then he saw Kong and hid just in time behind a huge boulder.

Kong was home!

His home was a huge half circle of rock. It looked as if it had been carved out of the side of the hill. At the bottom of it lay a deep black pool.

No streams or rivers flowed into this pool. Jack suddenly understood. The stream flowed *from* this pool.

But why was Kong staring down into the water like that? Something was moving! There was something crawling out of the pool!

It was a giant snake. Kong leaped back. He laid Ann down in a safe place. Then once again the great ape attacked.

Kong won the bloody battle. He tore the huge snake into pieces. He roared and beat his chest.

But Kong was getting tired. Now that his home was safe, he wanted food and rest. He picked Ann up again. Then he made his way up to a cave high above the pool. Jack was right behind him.

Kong put Ann down on a ledge near the cave door. Just then he heard the flap of wings. A giant prehistoric bird flew by. A new danger! Kong turned away from Ann. He climbed up a cliff above the cave and

threw out a mighty arm. The bird was his! Horrible screams and roars filled the air.

It was the chance Jack needed. He ran to Ann's side.

"Ann!" he called softly.

"Jack! Oh, Jack! I knew you would come."

Their hands touched in the dark. They held on to each other.

Jack leaned over the ledge and looked down. The black pool lay below them. In a flash he knew how they would get away.

Kong tore the giant bird apart with his teeth. He looked down and saw Jack and Ann. He roared with surprise and anger.

Jack pulled Ann to her feet. His arm went around her waist. "Jump, Ann!" he cried. "Jump!"

Chapter 11

Ann and Jack jumped into the pool. The water was warm. When they came up for air, Kong was charging down the mountain. Jack had just enough time to cry out, "Dive, Ann!"

Ann took a deep breath and dove underwater. The next moment she felt herself being pulled down. She was being sucked through a stone tunnel. The current was strong and fast.

Suddenly Ann shot out of the side of the mountain. Jack came tumbling right after her. The water carried them swiftly along like logs.

"We're going to swim all the way," Jack said. "Think you can make it, honey?"

"I can do anything, Jack, now that you are here," Ann said.

But it took all of Ann's strength just to keep her head above the water. Often she had to rest while Jack pulled her along.

They floated as much as they could and let the river carry them. The moon rose to light their way.

Far behind them they could hear Kong crashing through the trees. "Kong has to come by land," said Jack. "This river goes much faster. We're going to make it."

They reached the lake. Jack remembered the dinosaurs. "We'll go around the edge by land," he said.

They lost some time along the shore. The vines were thick. The trail was rough and dark.

They reached the stream again. They jumped in and swam for their lives.

At last they heard a rushing sound up ahead. "It's the waterfall!" said Jack. "We're almost there, Ann. It may be tough. But we'll go over the falls."

The water tumbled them together. Then once more they were pulled forward. The water shot them over the edge. They slid down the side of the cliff.

Their arms and faces were cut in the fall. But they did not care. For ahead of them was the stone altar.

Beyond the altar was the wall. And the gate was open. Jack picked Ann up and ran toward the light.

Lumpy saw them first. "Yoo-hoo!" he called. "It's Miss Ann. The mate's got her!"

The sailors ran for the gate. Denham got to Jack first. They all hugged one another and jumped for joy.

The sailors took Ann from Driscoll's arms. They laid her down on a pile of coats. They poured brandy down her throat. Lumpy began to dress her cuts.

One by one the natives came out of their houses. They stared in wonder. The woman of gold had returned!

Suddenly the drums began to beat again. The people began to chant.

"Kong! Kong! Kong!"

Denham looked up. "Of course!"

he said. "The Beast will come back! We have what the Beast wants. We have Beauty."

"Quick!" shouted Jack. "Close the gate!"

The sailors ran for the wall. The natives ran too. Jack pulled Ann toward the boats. Once again they ran for their lives.

Kong roared out of the jungle. His huge body towered over them in the moonlight.

The men could not shut the gate in time. Kong put his huge foot in the opening. Then he began to pound the gate with his fists. The gate flew into a thousand pieces.

The natives screamed and ran. Kong stomped on. There were more screams as he crushed people under his feet.

Kong saw Ann. He was determined to get his treasure back. He headed toward the beach. But the gas bombs got to him first. Denham stood alone on the beach throwing the bombs at Kong. The other men had run for their lives.

It took four bombs to bring Kong down. The great gorilla gave a last loud cry. Then he crashed to the sand.

Chapter 12

Weeks passed, and once again it was night in New York City. The crowds jammed Times Square. They spilled over for blocks in every direction. It seemed as though everyone in New York were there. They shoved and pushed, trying to get a good look.

High above them hung a giant sign.

KING KONG
The Eighth Wonder
of the World

A big fancy car crawled through the crowd. The car made its way to the back of a big theater. It pulled up at a side door. Ann, Jack, and Denham got out.

They did not look like the same people. Those who had risked death on Skull Mountain Island. Ann was dressed in a beautiful gown. Driscoll and Denham wore evening suits.

Denham was happy. "Ten thousand dollars at the box office!" he said, rubbing his hands together. "Kong is going to make us rich."

"Kong's making Lumpy rich too," said Ann. They all laughed. The old man had become a favorite of the newspaper reporters. Ignatz was the most famous monkey in New York.

People crowded into the theater. Soon there was not a seat left. The lights went down. Denham took the stage.

"Ladies and gentlemen!" he cried. "I'm here tonight to tell you a strange story. So strange that no one will believe it. So I have brought back living proof. The beast you have all been waiting to see. The Eighth Wonder of the World. The mighty—King Kong!"

The curtains opened. King Kong appeared before them. But he was king no longer. The monster was kneeling in a great steel cage. Chains bolted him to the floor. Only his head was free.

Kong looked out at the people. His eyes were angry, yet sad. The people clapped and cheered.

Denham held up a hand. "There is the Beast. Now I'd like you to meet Beauty—the bravest woman in the world. And the man who saved her from the Beast. Miss Ann Darrow and Mr. Jack Driscoll!"

Ann and Jack came up on stage. The newspaper reporters rushed forward. Lights flashed and cameras clicked. Then Kong saw Ann.

There was a low growl from the cage. People in the audience gasped with fear.

"Don't worry, folks!" called Denham. "Those chains are made of chrome steel! Move closer to the cage, Ann. And smile. Let's get Beauty and the Beast in the same picture."

The lights flashed again.

Kong stood up. His great head hit the top of the cage. The bars flew loose! Then Kong's great hands began to rip the chains from his body. Nothing would stop him from getting Ann back.

Kong roared.

The people screamed and ran for the doors. Driscoll and Ann ran for the stage door. It slammed behind them.

"To my hotel!" cried Jack. "Right over there!" They ran. The hotel door closed behind them just as Kong reached the street.

Kong crashed into the hotel lobby. A cop emptied his gun into Kong's chest. The gorilla didn't feel it. He crashed through the walls of the hotel and into the street.

Now Kong climbed the side of the hotel. He spotted Ann through a window. This time Jack could not save Ann. The huge black arm reached in the window and grabbed her. Once more Kong swung Ann onto his shoulder. Then he leaped.

The crowd below saw him bounding across the roofs.

Jack pounded down the stairs. He met Denham coming up. "Kong got her!" Jack cried. They ran for help.

All the sirens in the city seemed to be in on the chase. Police cars and fire trucks screeched around the corners. Above them Kong was traveling fast.

"He's headed for Thirty-fourth Street," said Denham.

"The Empire State Building!" Jack cried. "It's the highest place in town! That's where he'll go!"

The crowd ran madly. The people stopped and looked up, amazed.

There, far above their heads, King Kong was climbing straight up the Empire State Building.

"We can't shoot!" cried a cop. "He's still got the woman!"

"I've got an idea!" Denham said. "Let's send planes after him. Maybe the planes can finish him off without hurting Ann." The cop nodded and ran to call the airport.

Driscoll dashed to another cop's side. "Give me that machine gun," he snapped. "Don't worry, man! I know how to use it!" He grabbed the gun and ran for the elevator.

Kong got to the top just as the planes came into sight. Their red and green lights came blinking toward him. He turned to face these strange new birds.

But first Kong very gently laid Ann down between his feet. Then he stood up, beat his great chest, and roared.

Ann slowly backed away from the edge of the building. She hoped to escape through a small window behind her. But she could not keep her eyes away from Kong's last battle.

The planes swooped down. Kong's arm flew out. His fist hit the first plane. It burst into flames.

But the second plane got Kong. A burst of gunfire hit the gorilla in the chest. Then the third plane zoomed in. Then the fourth. Again and again the planes circled around.

Kong fought bravely to the end. But soon he began to stumble. He turned slowly and looked down at Ann with great sad eyes.

Kong stood up straight and tall. He beat his chest. He gave a last mighty roar. Then Kong toppled and fell to his death.

Jack ran out and swept Ann into his arms. "Ann! Ann! It's all over!"

Ann hugged him and cried.

Down below, the people stared at the body of the great Kong.

"Well!" said the cop. "That was a sight. He fought like a hundred men. But the airplanes got him."

"The airplanes didn't get Kong," answered Denham. "It was Beauty who killed the Beast."

The cop shook his head. What was this guy talking about? These movie people were crazy. That was the only word. Crazy.

Judith Conaway is a full-time free-lance writer and all-around creative person. She specializes in educational and audiovisual materials, and has also written two other Step-Up Classic Chillers: *Mysteries of Sherlock Holmes* and *20,000 Leagues Under the Sea.* She is also a weaver, a puppet maker, and the author of three crafts books. Ms. Conaway lives in Rhinebeck, New York.

Paul Van Munching has illustrated covers for several science fiction and fantasy books. He also illustrated *Dr. Jekyll and Mr. Hyde,* another Step-Up Classic Chiller. Mr. Van Munching lives in New York City.